ELLI W

Swashbuckle Lil

and the Jewel Thief

MACMILLAN CHILDREN'S BOOKS

ILLUSTRATED BY LAURA ELLEN ANDERSON

First published 2017 by Macmillan Children's Books
an imprint of Pan Macmillan
20 New Wharf Road, London N1 9RR
Associated companies throughout the world
www.panmacmillan.com

ISBN 978-1-5098-0884-7

Text copyright © Elli Woollard 2017
Illustrations copyright © Laura Ellen Anderson 2017

1 3 5 7 9 8 6 4 2

A CIP catalogue record for this book is available from the British Library.

Printed and bound by CPI Group (UK) Ltd, Croydon CR0 4YY

*For the wonderful children of
Heathmere Primary School*
E. W.

*For Charlie, a swashbuckling
agent and super person! xxx*
L.E.A.

The Jewel Thief

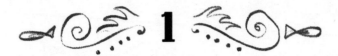

Normaltown School was a dull sort of place.

Nothing went on all day L O N G.

'It's always the same,' the children complained,

But, actually, there they were wrong . . .

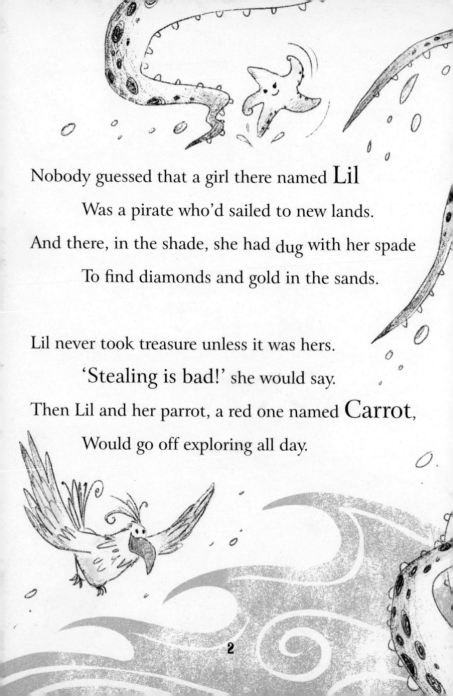

Nobody guessed that a girl there named Lil

    Was a pirate who'd sailed to new lands.

And there, in the shade, she had dug with her spade

    To find diamonds and gold in the sands.

Lil never took treasure unless it was hers.

    'Stealing is bad!' she would say.

Then Lil and her parrot, a red one named Carrot,

    Would go off exploring all day.

But if danger appeared in the winds and the waves,

Then Lil was as **bold** as could be.

She tackled big squid in the depths where they hid.

'Nothing,' she'd say, 'can scare ME!'

3

Yet even a pirate must learn how to read,

So that is why Lil sat in class.

But she daydreamed of whales,

and lightning-lashed gales,

And waters that glimmered like glass.

Miss Lubber, her teacher, would say to her, 'Lil!

Why is there sand on your chair?

Look at your shirt! It's covered in dirt,

And there's seaweed all over your hair!'

Then one day Miss Lubber said,

'Class, I've got news.'

'Oooh!' said the children. 'What is it?'

'Today,' said Miss Lubber, 'we'll all go away

On a wonderful, interesting visit.'

'This museum,' she said, 'will be ever so fun.

It's an **excellent** place for a trip.

We'll see famous old art, and the very best part

Is a hundred-and-ten-year-old ship.'

MUSEUM THIS WAY

'Ahoy!' shouted Lil. 'I know all about boats!'

But Miss Lubber just said, 'Come along.

Now, Lil, please be good and behave as you should,

And nothing at all will go wrong.'

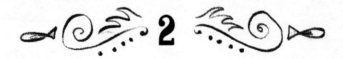

2

The museum was huge. 'Carrot,' said Lil,

'Just look at this place – it's so cool!'

But Miss Lubber said, 'Lil, I have told you:

STAND STILL.

Now, children, remember this rule:

'The stuff in museums is valuable art;

Just think of the millions it cost.

No touching, no reaching, no squealing or screeching,

And don't run around or get lost.'

'All of this stuff is like treasure,' thought Lil.

'It's really expensive and old.

And look! Here's a **ring** that belonged to a **king**,

With rubies and emeralds and gold.'

But the children said,

   'Miss, it's so BORING in here.

   Where's that big ship, like you said?'

'Over here,' said Miss Lubber, and everyone cheered

   As they ran through the doors straight ahead.

Miss Lubber was telling the class to be good.

'Listen,' she said, 'and don't talk.

We LEARN when we're here – is that perfectly clear?

But wait . . . What on earth was that squawk?'

'Shhh,' whispered Lil. 'Carrot, be good!

I told you – be quiet, don't chatter!

Don't flutter, don't speak, don't flap and don't shriek.

But hang on a sec – what's the matter?'

Then all of a sudden Lil let out a gaSp,

As she stroked her pet bird in her bag.

For right on the tip of the mast of the ship

Was Stinkbeard's filthy old FLAG!

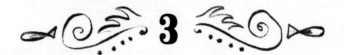

Stinkbeard was feared by all pirating folks.

He'd always, yes, *always* been mean.

There were bugs in his beard and his face was

all smeared

With the mouldiest food ever seen.

'Whatever old Stinkbeard is up to,' thought Lil,

'It's bound to be something that's **bad**.

He's always invading and looting and raiding;

He's foul, he's revolting, he's mad!'

'Miss Lubber!' Lil called. 'Ahoy, over here!'

But her teacher said, 'Lil, pay attention.

I've told you: don't shout when we're out and about,

Or else I will give you detention.

'Now hurry up, class – it's time for your snack.

 We'll all sit and eat it outside.'

But Lil muttered, 'No, I'm not going to go.

 Quickly now, Carrot, let's hide!'

A large wooden barrel was right by the ship.

 Lil said, 'Let's spy from in there.

Stinkbeard won't know that we're here. Yo ho ho!

 We'll JUMP OUT and give him a scare!'

'Won't Stinkbeard be shocked by my plan?' giggled Lil.

'But wait! Are those footsteps I hear?

They're *clop-clop-clop clopping*, and still they're

not stopping,

Oh no! They sound dangerously near!'

Then the barrel was tipping, and sliding and slipping,
And starting to swing and to sway.
'What's happening?' thought Lil. 'We're going downhill!'
The barrel was rolling away.

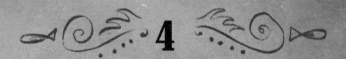

4

Down, down Lil rolled, yelling, 'Stinkbeard, you rat!

I will get you for this, just you see!

You revolting old crab! You can snatch, you can grab,

But you'll not make a prisoner of **ME**!'

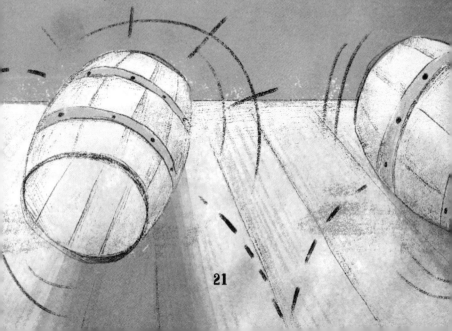

The barrel slowed down. Lil tried to climb out,

But the lid was locked shut with a snap.

And a voice said, 'I WILL take you prisoner, young Lil!

Aharrrr! Now you're caught in my trap.'

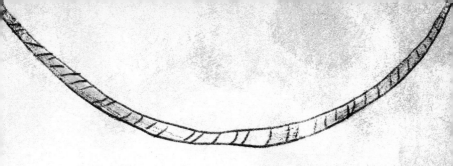

Lil bashed on the lid with a *bang, bang, bang, CLANG!*

But Stinkbeard just snorted and laughed.

'I won't let you go and escape, no, no, no!

You'll never get out – I'm not daft!'

'Later today I will burgle this place,

And grab an exhibit or two.

I'll steal that old ring that belonged to a king,

And there's nothing at all you can do.'

'Carrot,' said Lil as the minutes ticked by,

'I think Stinkbeard's having a kip.

His snoring's like THUNDER. Now, listen, I wonder . . .

Perhaps we can give him the slip.'

She whispered some words

in her pet parrot's ear,

Then Carrot pecked hard at the lid.

The holes grew and grew

till the lid broke in two,

And out Lil and Carrot both slid.

26

PIRATE SHIP EXHIBIT

OLD KING'S JEWELS

'Stinkbeard's a slimy old thief!' muttered Lil.

'Carrot, we must stop this crime!

I'm sure that we can and I've thought of a plan,

But hurry – there isn't much time!'

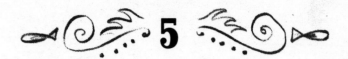

5

In the very next room was a case of old clothes

       That were once worn by little princesses.

There were shoes, there were boots, there were coats,

       there were suits,

       And a dozen or so frilly dresses.

She pulled on a dress saying, 'Here's our disguise.

       Listen now, Carrot, my mate.

We'll be statues,' said Lil. 'We must just keep still,

       And all we can do now is w a i t .'

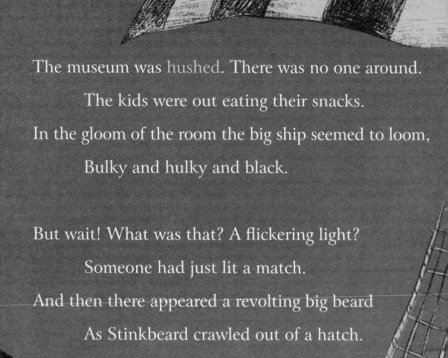

The museum was hushed. There was no one around.

 The kids were out eating their snacks.

In the gloom of the room the big ship seemed to loom,

 Bulky and hulky and black.

But wait! What was that? A flickering light?

 Someone had just lit a match.

And then there appeared a revolting big beard

 As Stinkbeard crawled out of a hatch.

The pirate crept to the edge of the ship,
And swung himself over the deck.
He looked all around, then said,
    'Wait! What's that sound?
    There's somebody in here. Oh heck!'

'It's only a statue!' said Stinkbeard. 'Oh phew!

For a moment I thought it was real!

And a stupid stuffed bird? Hee hee, how absurd!

Aharrrr! Now I'll go off and steal.'

The lock on the case was quite easy to pick.

'Oh ho!' Stinkbeard said. 'I'm the best.'

But just as he grabbed at the king's ruby ring,

A voice squawked,

'You're under arrest!'

6

'Heeeeeelp!' Stinkbeard shouted.

'That parrot just spoke.

But how can a stuffed parrot talk?

And that statue is moving towards me,' he screeched.

'What's happening? A statue can't walk!

'They're demons! They're devils! They're ghosties!

They're ghouls!

They're coming to get me!' he said.

'That bird bit my bum! I WANT MY MUM!'

And quickly he turned and he fled.

'After him, Carrot!' the 'statue' cried out.

    'Tickle him, quick, with your wing.

We'll hunt him and chase him! We'll hound him

        and race him!

    We must make him drop that old ring!'

They zipped and they zoomed through the halls

        and the rooms,

    W h i z z i n g along at top speed.

They darted and dashed in a blur and a flash,

        But Stinkbeard was still in the lead.

'STOP!' yelled the guards as they woke

from their snooze.

'Hey, what on earth's going on?'

And puffing and panting they joined in the chase,

But Stinkbeard seemed to have gone.

'You scumbag!' yelled Lil. 'You're scared – is that it?

Is that why you've just disappeared?'

Then she stepped on a rug, but it gave a small tug,

And she came face to face with . . . **a beard!**

'Arrrrrr!' Stinkbeard cried. 'You'll never stop *me*!

I've grabbed you and nabbed you at last.

This treasure's all mine, you revolting young swine!'

But Lil simply said, 'Not so fast!'

7

Lil whipped out the laces from both of her shoes,

　　Then tied Stinkbeard's legs good and fast.

She tied his hands too, then she cried out, 'Woo hoo!

　　I've finally caught you at last!'

'Huh!' Stinkbeard said. 'I'll soon get away,'

　　But he started to stumble and slip,

Then he tumbled – *ker-thwack* – fell smack on his back,

　　And the ring slithered out of his grip.

PA-DOING

The laces went *SNAP*, and off Stinkbeard ran,

Yelling, 'Ha! I am out of this place!'

Then Lil grabbed the ring that belonged to a king,

And she put it right back in its case.

Then all of a sudden Miss Lubber came up,

And her voice was a horrible hiss.

'All of this mess! You made it, I guess?

Yes, WHAT is the meaning of THIS?'

Lil tried to explain, but Miss Lubber said, 'Child,

That's the silliest thing that I've heard!

A pirating crook and a ring that he took?

I don't believe one single word!'

'Really!' thought Lil as the class all marched home.

'Teachers are always unfair!

I acted in time to prevent a huge crime,

But Miss Lubber – she just doesn't care!'

So Lil got in trouble at school yet again,

And nobody, nobody knew

That Lil was a hero, a swashbuckling hero,

And all her adventures were true.

Party, Me Hearty!

TO
BILL

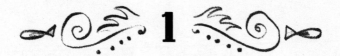

1

Lil and her parrot were strolling along

When Lil whispered,

'Carrot, me hearty,

Don't make a sound and don't flip-flap around.

Remember,

we're off to Bill's **PARTY.**'

'Today's my friend's birthday,' Lil said to her pet.

'We must behave nicely, all right?

His mum will be there, so we'll have to take care

To be ever so good and polite.'

But Lil sighed to herself as she walked past the shops,

'I'd rather be out on the waves.

I'd dive in the sea and catch fish for my tea,

Then roast it on campfires in caves.

'A party's not nearly exciting enough;

You just sit around playing games.

There aren't coral reefs, or bad pirate chiefs,

Or sea-monsters breathing out flames.'

She stomped past the park, she stamped past her school,

And on to her friend's big front door.

But then she said, 'Wait! What's this by the gate?

A poster? And what is it for?'

STOLEN:
OLD COINS PRICED
AT MILLIONS OF POUNDS,
A GLITTERING GLIMMERING
HOARD.
THEIR OWNERS CONCERNED
AND THEY MUST BE
RETURNED.
FIND THEM AND CLAIM
A REWARD.

Stolen: old coins priced at millions of pounds,

    A glittering, glimmering hoard.

Their owner's concerned and they must be returned.

    Find them and claim a reward.

'Stinkbeard!' said Lil. 'I bet it was him!

    That wicked old pirating chief!

We'll find where that brute has concealed all this loot,

    And then we will catch that foul thief!'

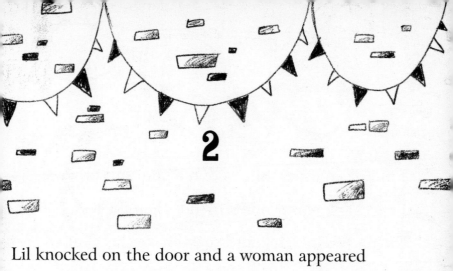

2

Lil knocked on the door and a woman appeared
      Looking terribly tidy and neat.
She peered down her nose at Lil's scruffy clothes,
      Then barked, 'Come inside. Wipe your feet.'

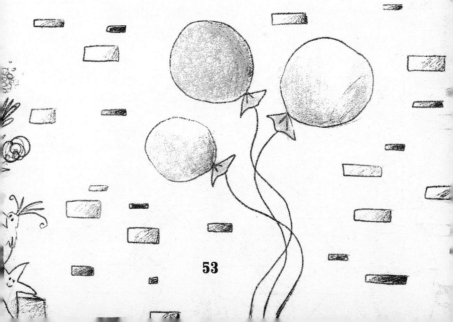

'I'm Bill's mother,' she said in a grim sort of voice.

'You're one of his friends then, I guess?

The party's in here, but I must make this clear:

No shouting, and don't make a mess.'

'Oh dear,' whispered Lil to the bird in her bag.

'Isn't she horribly snooty?

But we still must be good and behave as we should,

So come along, Carrot, me beauty.'

The rest of Bill's friends had already arrived.

They saw Lil and said, 'Oh, hello!'

Bill's mum gave a glare and a mean sort of stare

When Lil replied, 'Hey! Yo ho ho!'

'Children, it's time for some games,' said Bill's mum.

'But listen to me, girls and boys.

No jumping, no bumping, and please, kids,

no thumping.

Be gentle, and not too much noise.'

'Huh!' muttered Lil, as Carrot hopped off.

'It's as boring as boring could be!'

And she thought of the hoard and

the promised reward.

'Where,' murmured Lil,

'could it be?'

Then all of a sudden her parrot returned,

And he dropped something –

PLOP

— in her lap.

'Look what I found,'

Carrot squawked, 'on the ground.'

'Oh!' muttered Lil.

'It's a map!

'What does it say? The ink is all smudged.

But one thing is perfectly clear:

This map leaves no doubt that old Stinkbeard's about,

And the coins that he stole must be near.'

3

When no one was looking Lil slipped off outside.

'Carrot!' she said. 'Come and look!

Footprints, I think, and they pong! Yes, they stink!

I bet they belong to that crook!'

'But whose prints are these? Not human at all . . .

Right over here, by this rock.

It's not fluffy paws,

but something with claws –

It must be old Stinkbeard's

pet **CROC**!'

'We're in danger!' cried Lil. 'If that croc is around
　　　　It will gobble us up for its lunch!
It's scaly and green and it's horribly mean,
　　　　And will grind up our bones with a crunch!'

'Stinkbeard, I know that you're hiding,' called Lil.
　　　　'Show me your face, if you dare!'
And she looked all around, but there wasn't a sound;
　　　　Stinkbeard, it seemed, wasn't there.

'That scumbag will come for the treasure,' said Lil,

'But we'll have to make sure we're there first.

Or else he'll come back and he's sure to attack.

Oh, that scoundrel is really the worst!'

Lil snatched up a spade and she dug and she dug.

The hole in the lawn became vast.

But what was that gleaming, and golden and beaming?

Could it be treasure, at last?

'The coins!' shouted Lil. 'I know that they are!'

And she started to scrape off the mud.

'We've done it!' cried Lil, and turned

cartwheels, until . . .

Footsteps came up –

thud, thud, THUD!

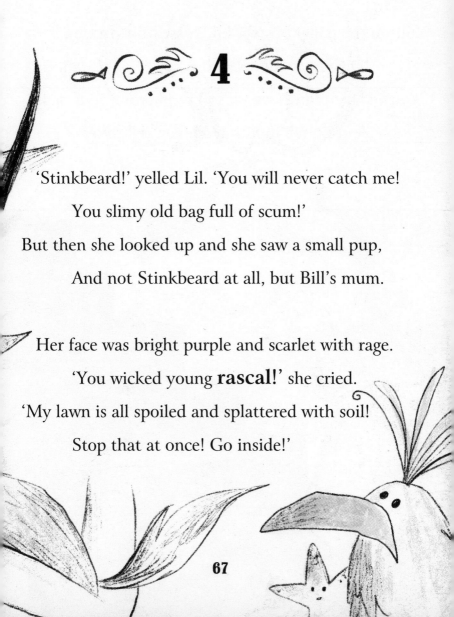

4

'Stinkbeard!' yelled Lil. 'You will never catch me!

You slimy old bag full of scum!'

But then she looked up and she saw a small pup,

And not Stinkbeard at all, but Bill's mum.

Her face was bright purple and scarlet with rage.

'You wicked young **rascal!**' she cried.

'My lawn is all spoiled and splattered with soil!

Stop that at once! Go inside!'

67

'Sit on the naughty step, Lil,' hissed Bill's mum.

'Digging I will not allow!

You've been horribly bad, so I'm phoning your dad,

And I'll tell him to fetch you right now!'

'That beast will come back for the treasure,' thought Lil,

'And nobody else even cares!

But that scoundrel will see

that a step won't stop ME!

But hang on – what's that on the stairs?'

'Seaweedy slime!' Lil said to herself.

'Right on each step – a whole trail.

And there at the top, where it comes to a stop,

Is the tip of a **scaly green tail!'**

Lil leaped up the stairs, three at a time,

And gave the most ear-splitting yell.

'Stinkbeard, I bet you I'm going to get you!

And may I inform you – you smell.'

70

Lil searched in the bedrooms; she peered under beds,

In wardrobes and drawers of all sorts.

But the tail and the beard had just disappeared.

'Perhaps in the bathroom?' Lil thought.

5

The crocodile grinned as it lounged in the bath,

Painting its wicked long claws.

Its black eyes were beady; its smile was greedy;

It saw Lil and opened its jaws.

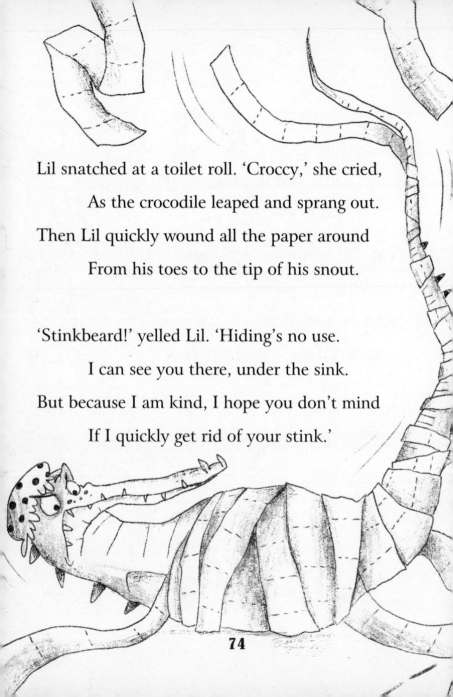

Lil snatched at a toilet roll. 'Croccy,' she cried,

As the crocodile leaped and sprang out.

Then Lil quickly wound all the paper around

From his toes to the tip of his snout.

'Stinkbeard!' yelled Lil. 'Hiding's no use.

I can see you there, under the sink.

But because I am kind, I hope you don't mind

If I quickly get rid of your stink.'

A big can of shaving cream stood on the floor.

Lil grabbed it and said, 'Now, take that!'

The foam spurted out in a huge frothy spout,

And landed on Stinkbeard –

kerSPLAT!

'And now you could do

with a rinse,' shouted Lil,

Giving Stinkbeard a sweet little grin.

And she turned on the shower

with a switch marked

FULL POWER . . .

Just as Bill's mother walked in!

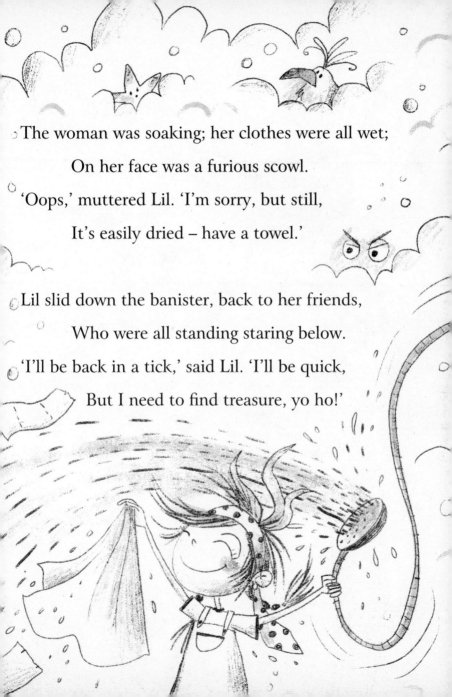

The woman was soaking; her clothes were all wet;

On her face was a furious scowl.

'Oops,' muttered Lil. 'I'm sorry, but still,

It's easily dried – have a towel.'

Lil slid down the banister, back to her friends,

Who were all standing staring below.

'I'll be back in a tick,' said Lil. 'I'll be quick,

But I need to find treasure, yo ho!'

6

Carrot was waiting for Lil in a tree.

He fluttered down fast in a flurry.

'To the treasure!' Lil cried as she darted outside.

'We'll stop that old brute if we hurry!'

But then she glanced up at a window above.

'A ladder?' Lil said with a frown.

It swayed and it shook, and *there* was the crook!

Stinkbeard was clambering down!

'Aharrrr!' Stinkbeard said. 'You silly young girl!

You're ever so small and so cute.

Just do as I say, and run off to play.

You won't get your hands on my loot!'

'Oh, really? We'll see about THAT!' shouted Lil,

As she tugged on a line full of washing.

Down it all fell, and Lil gave a yell:

'Stinkbeard, I think you need squashing!'

'Help!' Stinkbeard screamed. 'I'm buried alive!

These underpants want to attack me!

They'll bosh me, they'll beat me, they might even

eat me!

They're trying to thwack me and whack me!'

'Croccy!' he yelled. 'We must get away!

There seem to be murderous pants!

And now I am itching and

scratching and scritching.

Arrrrrr! They're all covered in ants!'

'Yo HO!' muttered Lil as Stinkbeard ran off.

'And now for the treasure – come on!'

So she dug, but then said, with a tremble of dread,

'Carrot, the treasure has gone!'

7

'Stinkbeard has taken the treasure!' yelled Lil.

'The rotten old scoundrelly scum!'

But a voice said, 'My dear, you're lying, I fear.'

And there on the grass stood Bill's mum.

'My dog found this stash of old coins here,' she said.

'Oh yes, I have got the whole hoard.

My clever young pup just dug them all up,

And now I will claim the reward.'

'Your dog?' spluttered Lil. 'But *I* found those coins!

I saw them and dug them up first!

Carrot,' she said, with a shake of her head,

'Grown-ups are really the worst!'

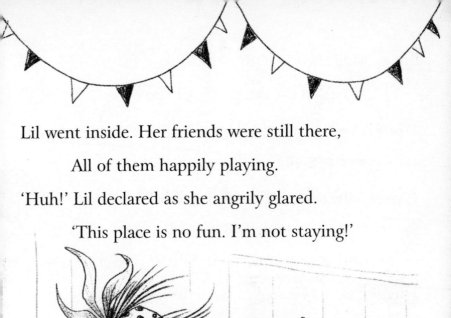

Lil went inside. Her friends were still there,

All of them happily playing.

'Huh!' Lil declared as she angrily glared.

'This place is no fun. I'm not staying!'

But passing the kitchen Lil looked and she saw

> The food for the party – a feast!

'Carrot, tuck in!' said Lil with a grin.

> 'We both deserve this much at least!'

'Look, there are coins made of chocolate,' said Lil,

> And Carrot squawked, 'Pieces of eight!'

Then he bit a big slice of something else nice,

> And said to Lil, 'Pizzas are great!'

So Lil went back home from the party that day,

And nobody, nobody knew,

That Lil was a pirate, a fearless young pirate,

And all her adventures were true.

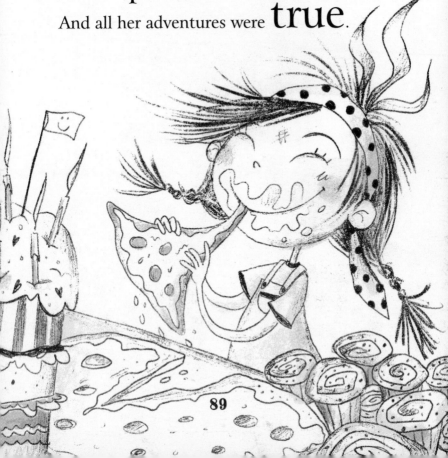

More fun from
ELLI WOOLLARD

For younger readers

For younger readers